The Kwanzaa Brunch, A Holiday Novella

DL White

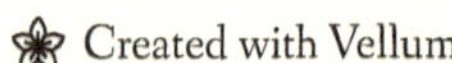 Created with Vellum

Foreward

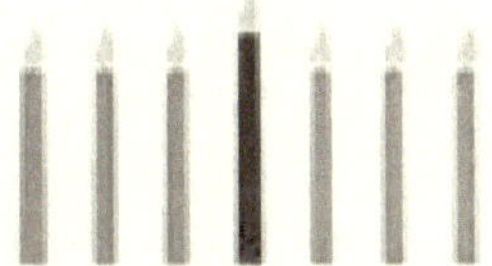

A fated brunch and an unlikely Cupid...

Sienna Charles is tired of the same old, same old. Same old job, same old city, same old friends. Same old men. Just when she's relegated herself to living Groundhog's Day romance edition, Booker LaSalle swaggers into her life, courtesy of an open position at Precision Software. He's new — to the company, to the city and, most importantly, to *her*.

Booker LaSalle is making a new life for himself. He relocated to an Atlanta suburb, leaving a stressful job and an ex-wife behind for a great job with growth potential. He's turning over a new leaf — no more falling for the first pretty woman that crosses his path... like the witty, gorgeous and obviously interested analyst at Precision. Everything about her tempts Booker to throw that "new leaf" plan out of the window.

Please note that if you have not read Unexpected, a holiday short, this book will spoil the ending for you! Pick it up **HERE**.

Chapter 1

Author's Note

Hello to my new and seasoned readers! It's a joy to be bringing a book to you this month! It took every ounce of fight, but I finally have my holiday short for 2019! She almost didn't happen, but I hope you adore Sienna and Booker because these two would. not. die.

A note that if you haven't read **Unexpected**, this story is going to spoil it for you! If you care about that sort of thing, go back and read it first. Meet Anthony and Faith and more importantly, Will and Saidah. (And since I get questions about how to pronounce her name, it's SAY-DAH or SAH EEH DAH. Either way works.)

Forge ahead if you don't mind, but you have been warned if you wanted to read the happy ending for yourself!

It is my deep wish that everyone has a pleasant, peaceful, happy end to the year and that plans for a productive 2020 are underway. I honestly have *no idea* what's coming from Books by DL White. It'll be some hotness, though, so BRING IT ON.

Please enjoy this tongue in cheek, light Kwanzaa romance. As always, if you loved it, drop a good word.
Merry Chrismahanukwanzaakah!
DL White

Chapter 2

Sienna

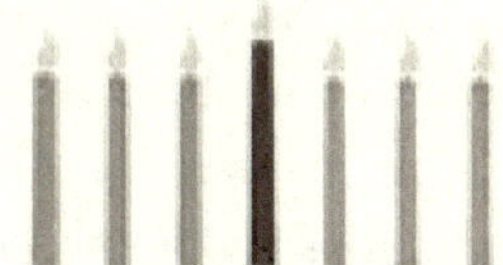

S ienna

Beee-boop. Beee-boop. Beee-boop. Beee-boop.

Aggressive lyrics and hard, driving beats from Complex Magazine's year end hip hop round up blasted through my headphones while I glared at the blinking, warbling object perched on the corner of my desk. My office line had been ringing nonstop for the past half hour.

I rarely picked up the phone, a well-known fact at Precision Software. Sales analysts were support staff, not customer facing, and the staff I supported would rather email or leave a voicemail. If they wanted to chat — which was rare, and that was *fine* — they knew how to find my office.

Anthony Thomas, lead sales consultant with the biggest customers and most complicated account profile, got great joy out of doing the opposite. He'd rather call than email and would keep calling until I picked up. I only put up with him because his wife was one of my best friends.

And because she was a chef. Not "a person who likes to cook" or that messes around in the kitchen. Faith was *Le Cordon Bleu*-Paris trained, and I was a big fan of a well-cooked meal. I could count the curves Faith had put on my hips since our college days.

Beee-boop. The phone lit up again like Christmas.

I seethed, punching the button to open up the line. "No," I barked, yanking off my headphones and slipping the telephone headset over my ear. I maneuvered the microphone, so it was in front of my mouth, the better to snap at him about blowing up my phone.

Anthony wasn't discouraged, as this was the standard Sienna Charles greeting. "You don't even know what I'm calling about."

"It doesn't matter what you're calling about. Did you forget where my office is? Or what that interoffice chat bubble means on your desktop? Or how email works? I'm *busy.*"

Anthony laughed, his cackles climbing to that pitch only dogs could hear. "You're so funny when you try to be hard, Sienna. For real, though. Are you coming down to—"

"Definitely no. Make that *hell* no."

"Come on. You know she does it to be nice."

"Do I look like a person who cares about that woman being nice? I fell for the bullshit last year and frankly, you're still on punishment because you didn't warn me about her."

Her was Zoraya Mason, the new CEO of Precision Software. She took over the company a year ago, after her father, Ezra, stepped down because of health problems. She brought her shiny new MBA and modern business strategies to Precision and implemented a host of changes, one of which was a Diversity and Inclusion Committee. While I applauded the observance of cultural and religious holidays represented by the staff, our new chief executive was overly eager to be one of the gang.

She wanted everyone, from the Vice President to the janitor to call her Zoraya, or Zo. She'd had her title removed from the website, her nameplate and her business cards. Zoraya loved employee gatherings and insisted on bringing a dish to contribute to the table.

But wherever her *Black Girl Magic* shone, it wasn't at the stove. Or the oven. Not even the refrigerator. The woman *could not* cook.

But she *really* wanted to and always tried. Trying not to hurt her feelings about it stressed me out.

"Zo has every department breathing down my neck right now. Her roasted goose frappe or whatever the hell she brought in for this fake woke Kwanzaa Brunch ain't it, Chief."

Anthony laughed again. "Hey, don't hold back. Tell us how you really feel, Sienna. You ain't got to eat, just come down. You know she'll be looking for you."

"And watching to see if I eat any of what she brought."

Like her food would pass these lips.

"I don't even know why you're fighting this. Zo will come find you. And I'm not lying for you again, like I did at the Bashover."

I moaned aloud, recalling Zoraya's attempt at a *light-hearted* Passover gathering, featuring her inedible Matzo

Ball soup. It was a river of dough. Anthony had been grilled about where his *friend* was and asked to encourage—more like bully — me to come down and support our Jewish employees.

"Fine. I'm not eating anything. I might have some punch, if it's store-bought. I'm not drinking anything served out of a bowl with orange slices in it. There's no telling what animal did the backstroke in that thing when no one was looking. Then I'm sneaking out, and you will not give me shit about it."

I pouted, gliding my fingers along the thin, sleek keyboard to lock my computer. "And Faith owes me pecan sweet rolls for this."

"I'll alert her to your demand. Meet you down there," he said, then hung up, cutting off any further argument.

Rolling my desk chair back, I stood, surveying the small but tidy office that I called home for fifty hours a week. The desk and single guest chair took up most of the closet sized room. Two monitors flanked the laptop locked into the dock at the center of the desk. An external keyboard, wireless mouse and desk phone took up nearly every inch of space left, so I used a side table to hold files, notepads and a collection of pens.

Posters, black art, and popular, snappy sayings covered the walls. The room was a study in my personality—techy with a sharp tongue and *take no shit* attitude.

I tapped the silver-plated lamp that I preferred over the fluorescent bulbs, then grabbed the hoodie that I kept folded over the back of my chair and pulled it on before stepping into the hallway.

I grumbled, like the overworked corporate drone that I was, but the past ten years at Precision hadn't been bad. Competitive salary, good people — chummy CEO who tries too hard notwithstanding, great benefits and amenities, all housed in an updated state-of-the-art building. Like a lot of software companies that popped up in the dot-com era, employees spent a great deal of time at work and the higher-ups believed in making that time as painless as possible.

I'd worked my daily routine down to rote, scheduled tasks, and now the process was a lot of the same thing every day, day in and day out. It was... comforting.

Eh, not really. I loved my job, but I was bored, and not just at the office. I'd had the same friends since undergrad at Albany State, lived in the same condo, shopped at the same neighborhood grocery store and ate at the same restaurants. I'd dated the same man ten times over; if not the same man, the same *type* of man. The definition of insanity was doing the same thing again and again, expecting a different result.

I was tired of the insanity.

I passed the break room, which housed a fully stocked vending machine and always smelled like burnt coffee, then waved at a few of my associates in the bullpen, an open office environment with low cubicle walls and bright overhead lights. It would not be unusual to see a beach ball bouncing from desk to desk or a meeting being held around the billiards table while a game was in progress.

Rounding the corner, I entered the elevator lobby and punched the button to call it. When the doors slid open, I stepped inside. Then I turned and assumed the position: arms folded across the chest, feet planted apart, stoic game face on.

Zoraya was not going to guilt me into eating her horrible ass food today. Bring it, Black Barbie.

Chapter 3

Booker

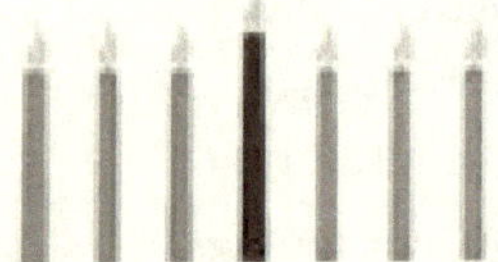

B ooker

"So, the company does this kind of thing often?"

I lumbered down the hall next to Anthony, my trainer at my new gig. Anthony was short and had that *happily married, my wife cooks every night* belly paunch, so he was moving slowly, more wandering the hallway than walking. He didn't seem to be in a hurry to get down to the main floor for this brunch everyone had been talking about.

"This kind of thing, like the Kwanzaa brunch?" He shrugged, stuffing his hands into the pockets of his jeans. "We didn't used to, but the new CEO is still trying to win us over. I guess the folks like it. We get paid to eat, especially since she has us in here the day after Christmas."

He threw a glare in my direction. "I'm normally on vacation, but she's changing some things up and we need to catch up. You need to be out in your territory in January. First quarter is when business spend the most money."

"Yeah, yeah. I remember you saying that a few times."

I rubbed dry palms together, eager to finish my training and conquer this new position. Precision was a powerful player in Business Management applications, and I was chomping at the bit, not only to blow this new job out of the water, but to make my mark in a different city. Double-X Systems, Tara Lasalle and Baton Rouge, Louisiana, were in my rearview mirror. It was full speed ahead, a whole new Booker Lasalle, from here on out.

I had lived in Atlanta long enough to sign the lease on my apartment, stock the cabinets with a few groceries and report to work. Training had been a long haul of endless days and paperwork, so a break for lunch and some social activity was most welcome. Not that Anthony wasn't personable, but I wanted to look at someone else's face for a change.

We rounded a corner to the elevator lobby and Anthony punched the down button. After a few moments, the doors slid open. A sour faced woman stood in the middle of the cube, her arms folded tightly across her chest.

"Ay, fam!" Anthony yelled. Of course, he knew her. Anthony knew everybody. He stepped into the elevator and held out a fist for her to bump it. "Make room! Damn."

She stepped aside with a grumble of "whatever," and uncrossed her arms, giving his fist a bump to complete the gesture. Her hoodie had large white block lettering that read *FUCK IT, WE'LL DO IT LIVE*, which made me laugh while increasing my appreciation of the atmosphere at Precision. They clearly didn't stifle an employee's personal sense of style.

I stepped in and shuffled to the other side of the elevator, putting her in the middle.

"You mad?" Anthony asked her, grinning.

"Nope," she answered, too quickly and sharply to not be upset. "I just hate office politics and schmoozing when I have shit to do. I'm backed up on accounts I need to update before we switch over to your new profile. I'm in the middle of month end and Zo has the finance manager on my ass about quarter close *and* year-end reports. She wants them before the first of the year. We never have to provide reports before the year is out—"

"You'll be fine," Anthony soothed. "It's not like you've never written a report before. It's an hour off. Bets on what Zo brought?"

"Only if we're betting food," she replied. "A Dulce de leche cake from your wife says whatever she brought is disgusting. I've already won."

"You know, I don't think Faith wants to be involved in our bets anymore. It creates work for her."

"That means you lose to me too often. She should make you be her sous chef or something."

"So I can mess it up?" He giggled. "And get on her nerves and get banned from the kitchen? Might be a good strategy."

"You have no skin in the game, Anthony. You bet wild because it means nothing to you."

I leaned against the wall of the elevator as it slowly descended, catching a few people on each floor, and watched the volley of these two, mesmerized. Her tongue was sharp, and she was quick-witted. Her voice struck a husky tone that rubbed me in just the right way. So did her deep brown skin, almond brown eyes and coke bottle shape — enough to grab onto and then some. Her short cut, dark at the roots, and platinum blonde toward the blunt ends that hung over her eyes was striking against her skin and a noticeable contrast to thick, plum colored lips.

Not that I was paying attention. I had a text message inbox full of angry diatribes as a lesson to never dip my pen in company ink ever again.

But I at least wanted to properly meet this woman.

I eyed Anthony over her head, but he was oblivious, deep into shit talking. He really wasn't going to introduce us?

I stuck my hand out, loudly clearing my throat and interrupting their banter. "Hey. I'm Booker LaSalle," I said, directing the rise in my voice to her, but cutting my eyes at Anthony. "I'm new to Precision. Anthony's training me."

She paused, her wide eyes rolling up to mine in surprise, like she hadn't noticed that I had been standing beside her the entire time. And maybe she hadn't, because Anthony's personality was large and just this side of over-bearing.

"Hey," she said, giving me firm pumps and then a squeeze before she let go. "I'm Sienna. I'm an analyst here. I didn't think I had seen you around here, but I didn't want to embarrass myself by asking if you were new."

"Sienna hides in her office. She barks loud, but she doesn't bite, so don't be scared."

"Shut *up*, Anthony," she snapped, huffing and rolling her eyes. I choked back a laugh.

The elevator thumped, emitted a muted *ding,* and the doors slid open. The cafeteria, a café and the social center were on the main floor. We followed the crowd gathering around the reception desk. Instead of the normal sign-in sheet and harried front desk staff, there was a steaming crock pot, a few stacks of paper cups and a tray of cookies.

People milled around, sipping what smelled like hot apple cider, and wandered toward the cafeteria, its double doors propped open. A sign hung above the entrance, decorated in festive holiday colors.

Happy Kwanzaa from Precision Software!

"Here we go." Sienna's shoulders squared up, her lips pressed into a tight line.

"Aight, so... what's the deal?" My gaze bounced from Anthony to Sienna and back. "Y'all seem scared or something."

"You'll see," said Anthony. He seemed to enjoy the anticipation a little too much. I was learning to be wary of that twinkle in his eye. The crowd thinned, and we neared a table.

And paused.

"Hm..." I scrubbed a palm down my face. Then gripped my chin and stroked the unshaven hairs that had sprouted. "What... I mean..."

"Exactly," said Sienna. "Just... what."

Chapter 4

Sienna

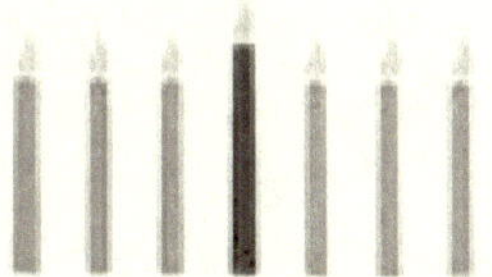

Sienna

Booker's eyes were wide, full of what I surmised was fear and loathing.

I stood between him and Anthony, struck speechless by a four-story red and green mottled monstrosity. It was so overwhelming, it had a buffet table to itself. The dull roar of conversation around us ground to a halt as more people entered the room and stopped at the table.

"Holy..." Muttered one of the engineers.

"Oh, dear God!" Yelped Regina, the receptionist.

"Ooh, look at everybody checking out my Kwanzaa cake! I was up all night working on this thing!"

Zoraya shuffled through the crowd to the front of the room in a red and green print dashiki dress and red patent leather sandals, her hombre bob lace front perfectly laid. Her lips, shellacked in Stunna red by Fenty Beauty, bent into a wide smile, beaming every ounce of the pride she must have conjured up to cart four tiers of brown, red and green cake into the building.

"I found this recipe on the Food TV site and decided to experiment," she gushed. "The base is Duncan Hines yellow cake. Then there's an apricot jam filling and chocolate frosting. And, to be holiday appropriate, I dyed the seeds and popcorn that decorate the outside."

She pointed at various globs and clusters, grinning wider. "A Kwanzaa cake should have a crunch to it," she declared. "I read that. Somewhere."

"I think she got lost on the recipe site," Anthony whispered, leaning over my shoulder.

"I had so much fun, I couldn't stop at one, so I made four. And I wanted it to be the centerpiece of our celebration, so I made tiers and... so, happy emoji!"

The room was silent, save the low rumble of people asking each other what she had just said.

"She means Umoja," I said, saving everyone the trouble of trying to figure it out. "It means Unity. For the first day of Kwanzaa."

"Right! Happy Kwanzaa!" Zoraya splayed her hands in a *ta-da* gesture. The crowd in the room responded with a smattering of claps and lackluster cheers.

I inched to the left, trying to get past the table so I wouldn't have to refuse a plate of the cake Zoraya was already cutting.

"Sienna!" *Fuck.* Too late. "Here's a slice for you! Thin, because I know you don't like to eat too many sweets."

I don't like to eat *your* sweets, sis.

Zoraya held out a slab of unappetizing brown goop, but froze mid handoff, uttering a surprised "oh!" as she took in the lettering on my hoodie. She seemed to force herself to smile through clenched teeth. I stared, daring the author of our Freedom of Expression in the Workplace policy to say a word about my choice of clothing.

"Well, that's... I...." Zoraya blinked, then unfroze and widened her smile. She shoved the plate toward me. "Cake?"

I didn't see any way to refuse the plate and not make a scene, so I took it, but with little enthusiasm. "Thanks, Zo. I'm gonna save it for later."

I turned, pushing my way out of the crowd to the next table, and prayed it held something store-bought and unopened. After rummaging several tables of dishes supplied by my coworkers, I scrounged up a sleeve of crackers and some cheese cubes, a few chicken wings from a restaurant container, a handful of chips, some grocery store cookies and a glass of punch, straight from the Minute Maid carton.

Anthony and Booker were across the room at a table dressed in a red and green checked plastic tablecloth, both plates loaded down with food. Now that I wasn't distracted by the shit show that was brunch, our newest employee could occupy my thoughts. Anthony hadn't said a thing about a new trainee.

Well, he could have, but Anthony had been long-winded since college. I tuned in and out.

So Booker was good looking. I mean, let me be honest. That man was *fine*. In a way that I wasn't used to.

Tall, but not a giant, like most of my exes. A rich reddish-brown skin tone, not a dark mahogany or a light caramel. Stocky, muscled but not in a *trying to get cast as the Black Panther* way. Booker was a strikingly handsome, random guy that I might pass on the street.

But I wouldn't expect to see him on the street, so I'd trip over myself on the double take.

More than his outward, Sterling Brown-esque appearance, it was the little things that niggled at that sensitive spot in the small of my back — the gentle strength in his hand when I shook his; the baritone of his voice and light accent when he spoke that told me he wasn't from around here.

I'd never made much of a habit of dating my coworkers, but allowances could be made for exceptional cases. When you've dated the same guy for ten years, *not from around here* made for an exceptional case.

I slid a paper plate with my paltry selections into a spot next to Anthony and dropped into a chair. "You have a death wish," I commented, directed at Anthony's plate. "You too," I said, angling my chin in Booker's direction.

"What I have," answered Anthony, around a mouth full of food, "is a system. See, I found out who was bringing what. And from that, I deduced who can cook and who has a clean kitchen—"

"There's no way you can know—"

"You can if you don't hide in your office all the time."

"I have the largest accounts, half of which are yours. I don't have time for potluck investigations."

Anthony laughed, biting off a chicken wing. "If you get to know people, you know whose food you can trust."

"I trust Faith's food, my mama's food, and my food. What about you, Booker? You don't seem scared."

"Well," he drawled, drawing out the word while stirring

a bowl of red beans and rice. "I figure it like this: I've eaten boudin, frog legs, alligator, cracklin, Tasso—"

"Do I want to know what Tasso is?"

"It's a delicacy. Made from hog shoulder. Usually we eat it with—"

"Nope, I don't want to know," I said, closing my eyes and holding up a hand to halt that description before he could say another word.

"Anyway, I figure if I can survive eating all of that on the regular, I can withstand some questionable food at a company potluck. Plus," he added, his eyes flicking up to mine while holding a spoon full of beans and rice. "I'm hungry. Sometimes you just got to be brave."

"Sometimes you got to have a will to live."

Booker laughed, then the bite of beans and rice disappeared into his mouth. He chewed vigorously, emitting a moan or a grunt every few seconds. "Whoever made these knew what they was doin'. I haven't had beans and rice like this since I lived with my Meemaw."

"Your... mee what?"

"Meemaw," Booker corrected. "Mimi. Mother Dear. Madea. What do you call your grandma, man?"

"Grandma!" answered Anthony, chicken wing in one hand and a half-eaten roll in the other. "How long since you saw her?"

"She's been gone a minute. She raised me since I was a boy. Mama had me young, left me with her." He paused, shaking his head, going back to his bowl. "Anyway, I need to know who made this so I can beg them for a big ol' pot on a regular basis."

"You could always ask my wife."

Bookers eyes lit up in the same way mine lit up about free food. "Oh, is she from Louisiana?"

"Nope, but—"

"Faith has never made a bad pot of food in her life," I interrupted, fawning as usual over my friend's culinary skills. "She could do red beans and rice with her eyes closed. I don't know about that Tasso thing you mentioned—"

"Now, that Tasso thing is tradition. It takes years to learn how to cook it."

"So give her time." I smiled, picking up a few Ritz crackers and a cube of cheese and nibbling on them. "Anthony, invite him to—"

Anthony nudged me sharply with his elbow, then cleared his throat and bowed his head, concentrating on clearing his plate. I took the hint and munched on a cracker.

"That all you're eating for lunch?" Booker asked. If he had noticed our exchange, he didn't let on. He eyed my plate, which didn't look or smell as good as his. "Hardly enough to tide you over for the day."

"I bring my lunch every day. I'll eat when I get back to my office. I only came down here because Anthony harassed me."

"Sienna doesn't like socializing." Anthony tilted his head toward me and rolled his eyes. "This used to be the type of place where you just keep your head down. Come in, do your work, do your thing, go home. Zoraya is all about the new way of doing business. Open concept, a family oriented, team-centered atmosphere. These lunches are her idea, and it's important to her that employees show up. If you're in the building and you don't come down—"

"You *will* come down." I finished.

"Wow," he drawled. "It's like that, huh? Zo sounds intense."

"It's not so bad," said Anthony. "Zo is smart. Got a good

business head about her. Her father taught her well. And with your help, we're going to top Double-X Systems next year. But she's also the boss, so you have to play the game."

"And the game is..."

"Stay employed," Anthony and I answered at the same time, then bumped fists.

Chapter 5

Booker

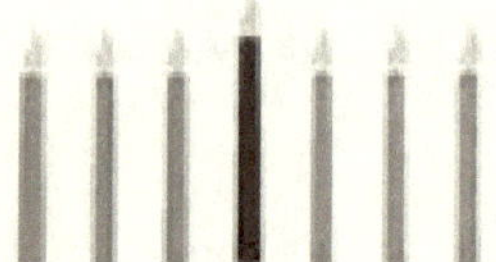

Booker
"One more manual to go over tonight, and then I need to bounce. It's my night to pick up my daughters from after school care."

Anthony handed me a tall paper cup and settled into the chair across from me. Precision valued Anthony, if the size and opulence of his office, not to mention his desk was any sign. The leather chair that he had been perched in during my training looked comfortable. Not at all like the stiff backed, cheaply upholstered, thinly padded guest chair that had been bruising my tailbone.

"Plus, I'm trying to get dinner out of the way before my Lakers play. You watching tonight?"

"Eh..." I shrugged. "I'm not a Lakers fan, man. I don't mind watching Bron, though." I took the cup and sipped, humming and nodding at the tasty brew. "That's good, as corporate coffee goes."

"Yeah, yeah. A lot of non-Lakers fans will watch tonight. LA was a good move. A tip for you though... never drink the coffee in the kitchen, man. It's strictly for the developers. They like it so thick a spoon could stand up in it."

He dry heaved, then swallowed a gulp from his own cup. "This is from the cafe downstairs. They use a special blend. Chicory or something like that."

I brought the cup to my lips and sipped more of the piping hot coffee. I licked my lips, savoring the perfect flavor. "So, uh... that woman we met earlier? The analyst? Your friend—"

Anthony was already shaking his head. "I'm gonna stop you right there."

"Stop me from what?"

"Asking about Sienna. I can't help you."

"How do you know I'm about to ask about her?"

"You have that look. You licked your lips; you did that thing with your eyes..."

"What thing with my eyes?"

"You leaned forward and did that thing we do when we're trying to be casual-like, but we're about to ask a friend about a woman. I'm not sure you're ready for her."

My eyebrows rose, mostly out of curiosity, but I was also a little offended. "You're what? Not sure I'm *ready* for her?"

Anthony shook his head and sipped more coffee, his tongue swathing his bottom lip.

"How do you—"

"Because I know Sienna. I've known her a long time. We went to school together, so when I say *fam?* I mean it. She's my wife's best friend. She's like a sister to me. Feel me? I'm not about to throw her into the mix with someone I don't know."

"Ay, I mean…" I had to pause, take in a breath, force a chuckle, because… seriously? "I'm not talking about marrying her. I'm just… asking about her."

"Why?"

"Pardon?"

"You heard me." Anthony stared me down, unblinking. He was mad serious about Sienna. I heard that, loud and clear. "Why are you asking about her?"

I shrugged, tossing my hands up. He had me. "I don't even know, man. She just seemed nice."

She seemed like an interesting person, but maybe I didn't need to be interested. My mobile phone buzzed inside the hip holster on my belt.

Another call from my ex rolling in.

He picked up a thick manual and dropped it onto the desk between us. "Back to work. You're on your own in January, and thinking about Sienna isn't going to help you with that."

"Doesn't she work on my territory?"

He wagged his head, frowning. "Nope. I get to keep Sienna. She'll be handling my accounts and you'll have your own analyst. Now, some of the clients I'm working with now will be yours. She'll transition them, so you'll get to know her soon enough, I guess. But not until you're trained, so…"

He tapped the manual, his brows hiked high on his forehead. I sighed, frowned, then reached for the manual. "Yeah. Back to it."

* * *

"Tara, you gotta stop blowing up my phone, then ghosting when I call you. Call me back."

I took the phone off Do Not Disturb and turned the ringer up loud before sliding it back into my pocket. Time to stop ignoring the former Mrs. LaSalle.

My first mistake was taking a job at her father's company. My second mistake was being hypnotized by green eyes and soft brown curls. My last mistake?

Marrying her. I was a pawn in a game that had been running for a long, long time.

Anthony had, as promised, rushed out hours ago to pick up his children. I stayed, camping out in a conference room since I hadn't been assigned an office yet, reviewing accounts, systems, and the way Precision did business. I was going to like this job. Essentially, this was a brand new experience, and I had every intention of eating it up.

Speaking of eating... damn, I was hungry.

By the time I pushed my way through the revolving glass doors at Precision, the sky had been dark for hours. It had also been hours since lunch and my stomach protested loudly. I walked toward my vehicle, clutching my belly and trying to decide whose drive thru I was about to crash. Behind me, I heard a derisive chuckle.

I turned to find Sienna keeping pace, a messenger bag slung across her body. "Lunch coming back to haunt you? I tried to warn you."

I knew what she meant. Office lunches weren't my thing either, but Anthony was my potluck sherpa. I trusted that he steered me away from anything questionable.

"Hey, Sienna." I greeted her with a nod, slowing down so she could catch up. We walked together toward the corner lot. She probably drove the two door Benz coupe, the only other car parked in that lot, a few spots away from my Range Rover. "I'm not feeling bad. I'm actually hungry."

"Unh huh. Look alive, though. Some of these folks might put some Mogwai in their dishes. You know, the kind that'll have your guts all unruly after midnight?"

I laughed, appreciating the teasing tone in her voice. It was... super sexy. "I hear you. So far, so good, though. Do they work you this late all the time?"

"Nah. It's just the season. Year end is busy for my department. The sooner I finish my reports, the sooner I'm done for the holiday. I'd rather stay and get it done."

"That's what I'm talking about." I nodded, grinning down at her. "Work ethic. I like it."

"It ain't no thang. I make a bonus off of those numbers, so don't get it twisted. I'm highly and personally invested."

"Anthony tells me you're going to be turning over some accounts to me, so we'll be working together a bit."

"A bit. Yeah."

"Looking forward to that."

Sienna paused, which made me pause, then turned around to face me. She still wore that hoodie she'd had on at lunch. She shoved her fists in the pockets and then bunched the front of the hoodie together, twisting the fabric from the inside.

"I was just thinking... I know a couple of places in the area where we could grab a bite. Even a few that serve creole dishes. Just as a welcome to the company. Wouldn't want you to go to sleep with visions of that ugly Kwanzaa cake in your head."

My mind popped back to my conversation with Anthony, which gave me pause. *You're not ready for her*, he had said. What exactly did that mean?

"Hey, no pressure," said Sienna, a softness in her tone.

"I know you're new to town and there's a lot of places to eat around here."

"You got that right," I agreed. "I have a feeling I'm gonna need to join a gym. And I'm grateful for food recommendations from a picky eater." I breathed a sigh of relief when she smirked and rolled her eyes. "So, what are we talking? Not Pappadeaux, right? You're not taking me to a chain, or some fake bougie cajun spot, are you?"

"Did you just — boy, no!" She cackled, tossing her head back. "Come on, now. I'd never take a person from Louisiana to Pappadeaux. Not that it doesn't hit in a pinch, but we have a few *authentic* spots around—"

BRIIIINNNNNGGGGGG....

I jumped, startled by the loud ring, then dug into my pocket for the phone. It was Tara calling me back at the most inopportune time, which was her way. I picked up the call, already irritated.

"Tara, hey. Hold on. Don't hang up." I glanced at Sienna with what I hoped was an apologetic smile. "I'm sorry, I've gotta take this. Raincheck?"

"Uh. Sure, No problem." She nodded, but her smile and soft tone had disappeared. She whirled around and walked away, moving quickly.

"See you tomorrow?"

I got no response, but she waved. I braced myself, then brought the phone to my ear as I approached my vehicle.

"Hey, Tara. Thanks for calling me back. So why—"

"Booker, who you talking to? Who are you seeing tomorrow?"

"Aight, first off..." I unlocked the truck with the key fob and tossed my bag into the backseat, then climbed into the driver's seat. "You need to chill on these questions. We haven't been legally married in over a year, so I don't answer to you. Why do you keep calling me?"

"I miss you."

She was pouting. Tara had a soft, baby voice, coupled with the downturn of bow lips she thought was seductive. Hell, maybe it was. It worked on me every time.

"I've been thinking, and... maybe the divorce was a mistake, Booker. We could just start over. We can try again, for real this time—"

"It wasn't a divorce, Tara. It was an annulment. Like it never happened. And how can we start over? You told me to forget you existed, forget we were married, to get out of your life. Remember that? Remember screaming that across the table at the lawyer's office?"

"Because I was upset! I didn't want to end our marriage."

"You should have thought about that before you signed those papers. I did exactly what you told me to do."

"And since when do you listen to me?"

"Ay, look, Tara. Today has been forty hours long, I swear. My stomach is about to turn in on itself, I'm so hungry. I need to get home so I can rest and be back at work early tomorrow. You be easy, aight? And stop calling me. We have no reason to talk."

Before she could argue, I ended the call and put the phone back on Do Not Disturb. I turned the key in the ignition and pulled out of the parking lot, just in time to see Sienna zip by.

Damn. I could have been having dinner with her tonight.

Chapter 6

Sienna

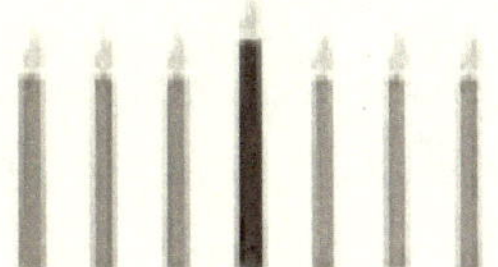

S ienna

"And so... who is Tara?"

Faith was only halfway listening while she whisked gravy in a saucepan. She hadn't even changed out of the white coat she wore at The Chef's Table, her catering company. How she could cook all day, then come home and cook for her family and still keep her coat a bright and spotless white was a feat of strength I could never achieve. I wore a hoodie to lunch because my chest caught food like nets caught shrimp.

"I need you to keep up," I ranted from my favorite spot,

a perch at the corner of Faith and Anthony's kitchen island, sipping on a glass of Miraval Provence Rosé while watching her make art with food. Her smothered chicken and rice already smelled delicious, and she wasn't even finished cooking.

"Okay, so you tried to ask him out, but he was talking to someone named Tara? Does she work at Precision?"

"No! He got a *phone call*. He called her Tara when he picked up the phone. Then he dismissed me, cause clearly he'd rather talk to some bitch than go out with me."

Faith burst into laughter. "Why's she gotta be a bitch, Sienna?"

"Because he would rather talk to her than go out with me!"

"Honey, I think that's enough wine for you. Anthony said you didn't hardly eat anything at lunch and I think it's going to your head."

I gulped the last swallow before she could take the glass away. "I ate. I just didn't eat what Anthony ate. Did he tell you about the cake?"

She snorted, still whisking and adjusting the heat. "He sent me a picture. Throw the whole cake away."

"Throw the whole brunch away."

"I mean, there is never a work appropriate occasion for a four tier cake."

Faith shook her head, then poured the prepared gravy over the baked chicken filets and slid the pan into the oven. "I'm going to let those cook together.... check my rice and my broccoli..."

She always mumbled to herself when she cooked, so I paid no attention while she lifted lids on pots and pans and cooking devices.

"Did he also tell you that you owe me a pan of sweet rolls? That was his bribe to even get me to go downstairs."

"Of course not. That's one of those things he pretends he forgot to tell me until we're in bed and I am half asleep." Faith turned then, grabbing a wine glass for herself and topping us both off before sliding my glass back over to me. With one hand, she unbuttoned her coat and used the other to deliver her glass to her lips.

She hung her jacket on the back of the chair next to me and climbed up, breathing a short, nearly inaudible sigh. On cue, Anthony wandered into the kitchen.

"Ay fam," said Anthony, giving me his usual greeting, accompanied by a fist bump. He grabbed a glass and poured the last of the wine into one.

"Hey, babe," Faith muttered through the kiss he dropped onto her lips. "Open a new bottle so it can breathe for a few minutes before dinner."

I watched Anthony follow her instructions, pulling a bottle from the wine fridge in the corner of the kitchen. As he bent over, I shook my head and clicked my tongue. "Faith, you need to tell your husband that married men don't wear gray sweats. They're single girl thirst traps."

"First," said Faith, her index finger in the air. "Keep your eyes in your head and off of my husband. Second... I *like* those sweats on him. Married women like to look. Thirst trap, *indeed*."

She sipped her wine loudly, then smacked her lips and winked at me. "When you get yourself a steady gentleman, you'll understand."

"I understand *now*. I've seen grey sweats before. I don't need to be looking at my best friend's husband's ass in them."

"In this house," shouted Anthony, while trying not to

laugh, "I wear the sweats that my wife bought me so I may cause her to thirst for me. And you've got a lot to say for someone that showed up at my house to eat after you only had cheese and crackers for lunch."

"I ate," I protested. "I just didn't eat that mess y'all ate. By the way, I saw Booker on my way out of the building, moaning like he was miserable. He said he was just hungry, but..."

"Oh boy," said Anthony, settling onto the stool next to me, while Faith hopped off to check the oven. "Here we go with this dude."

"Wait, who is Booker?"

"Booker is the guy I was telling you about! That was talking to Tara?"

"Oh, okay. The new snack at Precision with the shoulders and the chest and the swarthy accent. I kind of want to meet this *Booker*."

"I am not listening to this portion of this conversation," said Anthony.

"Turns out, he's Anthony's trainee. A trainee that he appears to have been hiding from the women in his life."

"I ain't hidin' nobody. I didn't know there would be so much interest in a new dude at work."

"And what do you mean, *here we go?*"

"You know exactly what I mean by *here we go*."

"No, I don't." I twisted in the chair, the better to see him. "Elaborate on *here we go*."

"Oh, Sienna..." Faith started, closing the oven door, then turning to face us both.

"What?" I asked, my gaze now bouncing from one to the other.

"You... you're just kind of a man-eater," said Anthony,

more quietly than he would normally make a declaration about me.

"I'm a *what?*"

"You heard me," said Anthony. "Not even *kind of* a man-eater. You're a literal, whole man-eater. You just gobble a dude up, spit him out. You're a player. You go through men like... I don't know, like a person who goes through a lot of things."

"Wait... what? Faith! Friend since college! You're co-signing this man-eater bullshit?"

"Well, honey..." She cringed, frowning. "You *are* a player. I mean, I love your dating stories, but you're getting up there in age."

"You say that shit like it's time to put me out to pasture. I date, yeah. I date *a lot*. I have a good time. How am I supposed to find a steady gentleman, as you put it, if I don't date? That makes me a player?"

"No," said Anthony. "That makes you a woman that dates. A lot. What makes you a player is ignoring a man who is worth your time to spend three nights a week with a dumbass who's just hoping to end up at your place afterwards."

"I don't know why you think I'm ignoring men worth my time. When I meet a man who is interested in more than hanging out and having sex, I'll explore that. Meanwhile, I'm cute and I'm a good time."

I crinkled my nose and stared at them both. "You mean I should go without sex because men are shallow?"

"Sienna, honey..."

"Uh uh! Don't Sienna honey, me! I thought we were friends."

"We are! It's just... sex is so meaningful when you're

with someone you genuinely care about, that you're building something with."

Faith crossed the kitchen to stand next to Anthony, who dropped a kiss on her cheek.

"You two make me sick," I grumbled into my glass.

Anthony's smug grin irritated me to my core. "This could be you, but you're a player."

"She buys you one pair of grey sweat pants and now you're a relationship expert. So, I'm not seriously pursuing The One or whatever. What does that have to do with Booker?"

"You work with him," said Anthony. "You can't just blow through a cute dude that you work with."

"We won't be working together after we move to your new account profile."

"You'll still see him. If things go south—"

"I don't burn my bridges. A guy I dated last year just got married. I went to his wedding and everything. Got them a real nice gift, like the adult I am. I'm happy as fuck for him."

Anthony chuckled. "Oh, you sound it."

"I *am*. I don't have an emotional attachment to the men I date."

"And that's the problem," said Faith, jumping in to point with a pair of cooking tongs. "The men that you would form an emotional attachment with are the ones you run from. You don't know how to handle those men. They're not into *cute and a good time* and you're scared you'll waste actual emotion and time and effort on someone who won't return them. That's always been your problem."

"You don't know me *or* my life," I mumbled. Then swallowed more wine and sulked, tracing the pattern of marbling on the island countertop.

But damn if they didn't just read me like the Sunday edition of the New York Times.

I'd known Faith and Anthony since my first day on campus at Albany State. I met Faith in the registration line and it turned out that we lived on the same floor of the same dorm.

We remained close, even after graduation, after their wedding and Faith's training in Paris. When they returned to Atlanta, and Anthony signed on at a fledgeling software company, he convinced them he needed an analyst to manage his accounts and sent my resume in.

The Thomas' had seen me through thick and thicker, through years of hot girl summers, through long and short bouts of dating. I was good for a fun and funny man story, but Faith was right. And so was Anthony. They'd seen me through more than a few relationships that would have had me living the blissfully mundane married life if I wasn't so chickenshit about feeling emotions and letting walls down.

My biggest fear was falling for someone as hard as they had fallen for each other, but having to do the walk of shame in Divorce Court years later. I wanted what they had. What my parents had.

And if I couldn't get that, guaranteed... I just couldn't risk my heart on a maybe.

"Booker asked about you after lunch."

I rolled my eyes up to Anthony, knowing my expression would compel him to finish his thought. To his benefit, he did so without me having to ask. He lifted and lowered his bulky shoulders, then added, "I told him I couldn't help him get to know you. He's not ready for Sienna Charles."

"Anthony!" I sputtered, half out of anger, half out of embarrassment that he had said that to Booker. About me. "So... great. He probably thinks I'm crazy, cockblocker."

"Maybe I did you a favor. He doesn't read as the type to hang out, hoping he'll end up at your place. I don't know if I want to play matchmaker here."

"It has all the markings of a nightmare," grumbled Faith, finally pulling the pan of chicken out of the oven. "Girls!" She called to her daughters. "Wash your hands!"

I climbed down from the bar chair and joined Anthony and Faith in our usual pre-dinner tasks. I set the table with plates and silverware while Anthony took care of milk for the girls and fresh pours for the rest of us. Faith set the pan of chicken and a bowl of rice and steamed vegetables at the center of the table.

"Why did you shush me when I said you should invite him to your New Year's Eve dinner? He's new to town, and he wasn't wearing a ring. He's probably not doing anything."

Anthony smirked. "I don't know that dude. And, like I said, I don't know if I want to be the connection between you two. I already know he'll gravitate to you, because that's what men do. I don't want to be responsible for whatever happens if you two spend time together."

"Saidah and Will are coming, right?" I brought up the third member of our friend group from college, who had met her husband at Christmas two years ago at the Thomas house. "They just got married and they're stupid happy."

"I don't know if I can take credit for them." Anthony grimaced, rubbing a palm over his closely cut hair. "I didn't even invite Will. And Saidah wasn't supposed to come to dinner that year—"

"Oh, please. You brag about bringing them together to anyone who will listen."

"Okay, yes. They're a success story. But they wanted

the same thing, and they were wide open to a relationship. Neither one of them were playing."

"You act like I set out to destroy men. I'm literally just out here dating. I'm just saying..."

Anthony passed the dish of smothered chicken to me. I served myself a generous portion, then added a spoonful of rice and some vegetables. Once everyone had been served, heads had bowed for grace and risen again, and the girls were chatting amongst themselves, Anthony prodded.

"You're just saying?"

"I'm not conceding that you're right. I think man-eater is a bit much. But I have noticed that my personal life is mundane. Repetitive. Groundhog's Day. Maybe I could try to get to know someone new, who's not the same as everyone I've.... *gotten to know*," I finished, watching the girls watching me out of the corner of my eye.

"Maybe we should invite him, honey?" said Faith, finally coming over to my side. "Like Sienna said, it would be a nice gesture. I know how you work and you've probably been driving him hard."

"Fine." Anthony tossed up his hands in defeat. "But I don't want to know if this goes sideways and I don't want you in my office or at my house talking about him either way. I do not want updates."

"I want updates," said Faith, grinning with her wine glass held aloft for a toast.

Chapter 7

Booker

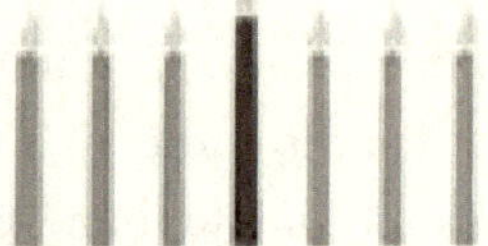

Booker

Much later than I'd intended, full of a gourmet burger, fries, and more than a few drinks from a restaurant down the street, I walked through my front door. There were plenty of good food spots to choose from, and I was making my way through them all. I dropped my bag and didn't give it another thought as I toed my shoes off. I left them at the door too and tossed my keys on the counter as I passed it.

I pulled my phone from my pocket, wincing at the number of missed calls, texts and WhatsApp messages. I dropped onto the couch, reached for the remote and kicked my feet up on to the coffee table, turning on the TV before thumbing a security code into my phone.

SportsCenter blared through the surround sound speakers as I scrolled past all the calls and messages from Tara. Eventually, I was going to block her, but for now, I supposed it made me feel good to know that she realized she'd lost a good man. Part of me loved to see her beg for me to come back.

The rest of me felt like shit for enjoying her pain. But then I knew she wasn't really in pain. She was fuming that she wasn't getting her way and couldn't use me anymore.

I popped open a running chat I had with my boys back in Baton Rouge.

> Ryan: What's up with Booker? Hotlanta ate him up?

> Greg: Ain't heard from Booker in days. He said he's in training or whatever. Anybody think he's training somebody on how to give him head?

> Jordan: #Sweatergawd G gotta bring up head every day.

> Ryan: A sign he ain't getting any.

> Greg: Y'all don't get none either.

> Jordan: I'm not part of that y'all. Ayanna... well. You know.

> Ryan: #also. I would tell y'all about Nalah's head game but you dudes gossip too much. Be telling all my secrets.

I chuckled, then tapped to post a reply.

> Booker: Only fools not from Atlanta call it Hotlanta, fool. You gotta kill that before you come through.

> Ryan: Ayyyyyy! What's good?

> Booker: Not much. Training is kicking my ass, but the gig is real good.

> Jordan: Hey, Book. Gig is better than 2X?

I grinned at the phone, taking pleasure in typing out my braggadocios response.

> Booker: In every way. A nice bump in salary, the mood seems good so far. Cafeteria and a nice coffee spot on the first floor. I get my office tomorrow. We had some kinda kwanzaa thing today, if that says anything. And no Tara Dupree.

> Jordan: That's the best perk right there.

> Booker: She's blowing up my phone tho.

> Greg: Still? Ain't it been like a year?

> Jordan: Got your hooks in her. Now she can't let go.

> Ryan: Told you not to marry that girl.

I had to give the nod to Ryan. He told me all the way up to five minutes before we walked into the courthouse.

Booker: Yeah, you told me that. You want a cookie or some shit for being right?

Ryan: Yeah. Send me my got damn cookies! She still big mad you signed those papers?

Booker: Big mad. Tryna come back and shit. Hell no.

Greg: You won, though. Going to the competition to make mo' money.

Booker: Yeah, I'm hype to push Double X off the leaderboard. Any way I can help Precision make that move, I'm on that.

Booker: What else is up out there? We bout to watch Bron run this game?

I laughed out loud, reading the day-to-day antics of my friends back home while we watched the Lakers stomp the Miami Heat. I missed my boys more than I thought I would, but I had to make the move that was best for me.

Besides, the plan was for all of us to leave Louisiana. Whoever left first would scope out a new spot, and if all went well, the rest would follow. Ryan and Greg would be in Atlanta within the year. Jordan was married and his wife would have to be dragged, kicking and screaming, from Baton Rouge.

Not a big deal, though. Ayanna was all about Jordan getting time away with his friends. We would see plenty of him.

Booker: Good game, good game. Bron makes a Lakers game watchable.

Ryan: You a sucka, Book. Just admit you're coming around.

Booker: Never. What you about to do?

Ryan: Nalah back there whining because I'm on the internet and watching basketball. I guess I gotta go be #boyfriendgoals.

Greg: Head.

Jordan: Gettin some?

Greg: Nawl. Just haven't mentioned it lately.

Booker: I'm about to turn in and let you fools clown Greg. Peace.

I didn't even wait for them to say goodnight. I locked the phone and heaved myself up from the couch, ignoring the empty water bottles and the glass I'd left on the coffee table, and headed down the hall to the bedroom.

I went into the master bathroom and turned on the shower, but a ping from my phone drew my attention. It was the standard text tone, which meant it was someone unfamiliar.

Anthony Thomas: You watch that game?
Bron is siiiick!

I carried the phone into the bathroom, catching the wrinkle creasing my forehead in the nearly steamed up mirror. Why was Anthony texting me so late? We could just talk in the morning. I shrugged and tapped out an answer.

Booker: Sure did. Enjoyed that win, even though I'm not a Lakers fan.

Anthony: A lot of non-Lakers fans sure watch a lot of Lakers games…

Booker: LOL. Just saying, I wasn't watching them before LeBron came to the team.

Anthony: I'm playing with you. You got plans for New Year's Eve?

I paused, thinking back to lunch when Sienna had suggested that Anthony invite me to something, but he had shut that down. Quickly.

Now I was getting an invite? Hm.

Booker: Not yet. I was thinking about heading back to Baton Rouge, but my friends all bought tickets to some big event with their girls.

Anthony: Well, no pressure, but my wife has ordered me to extend an invitation to our party. It's casual. Jeans are fine. I'll give you the details in the morning if you're interested.

I grabbed the collar of the polo I'd worn that day at the back of my neck and pulled it up and over my head, dropping it at my feet. My pants and boxers followed. Then, standing nude in my bathroom, the spacious, bland palate of the room blanketed in steam, I tapped out the question I was afraid to ask, that I had no business asking, with Tara still filling up my text message box.

Booker: Sienna gonna be there?

The text message dots bounced. Then paused. Then bounced.

Anthony: Yep.

Huh. Earlier he had said... but now... huh.

Booker: Is this a thing where you're asking to be nice, but I should refuse, cause it's gon' be some fuckshit?

Anthony: LOL! No, man. It's a nice time. And you want to taste my wife's cooking. She goes all out for holidays. I might could talk her into making you a pot of red beans and rice if it'll convince you to come out.

I nodded, giving a fist bump to nobody. I'd go through hell for red beans and rice.

Booker: Magic words. I'll talk to you tomorrow.

Anthony: Bet. Oh, and be early. Faith has catering jobs lined up until New Year's Eve so I'll be getting the house ready. I'm cutting out about mid-morning. We have a lot to cover.

Booker: Aight. Sounds good.

I set the phone down on the counter and stepped into the shower, smiling while I pulled the glass doors closed behind me. Something had changed. I could feel it.

Chapter 8

Sienna

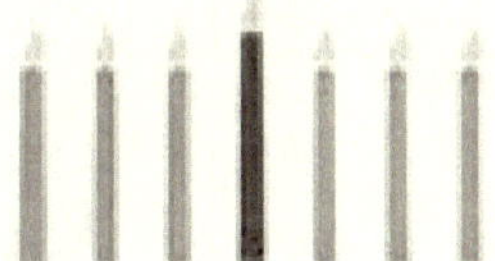

S ienna

"And! We! Are!"

With a flourish, I pressed the enter button on my keyboard, grinning as I watched the last of my reports fly off into the ethernet. Or somebody's mailbox. Anywhere but on my desk or on my to-do list.

Dooooone!" Arms outstretched, I sang out loud to no one.

I immediately flipped the music that had gotten me through the last working day of the year from my headphones to the small but powerful speakers sitting on my desk. It was well after hours on a light staff day. Anyone who was still hanging around burning the early evening oil deserved to be treated to good music.

Whitney Houston's golden voice trilled as she masterfully slayed every note change in her rendition of *Joy To the World*. I stood, knocking my chair back, miming direction of the Georgia Mass Choir, full and beautiful in the background. As the daughter of Lighthouse Baptist's long time choir director, I could at least pretend that I knew what I was doing.

Just as Whitney, backed by the choir, reached a fever pitch crescendo, the door to my office popped open and Booker stepped in. He was in dark rinse jeans and a long-sleeved, light blue t-shirt, but the unexpected pop-up made my heart drop to the pit of my stomach.

He was amused, evidenced by the grin that split his face. He dropped the folder he'd been carrying onto my desk, clapped his hands and began swaying in time as if he was in the choir I was directing.

I screeched in laughter that was way too loud, even for a quiet office. I reached for the keyboard to press the pause button.

"Whew!" I fanned myself, still giggling at his dancing. I'd worn an ugly holiday sweater to work — Zoraya's idea — and it was warm in the enclosed space. Also, my handsome *as fuck* new coworker had just joined me in a ridiculous song and dance in my office.

Booker took it in stride, not even breathing hard as he reached for the folder he had tossed onto my desk. "You'll have to excuse me. Ain't heard a good mass choir since Meemaw's funeral."

"You had a mass choir at your grandmother's funeral?"

"Oh, she had her home going all arranged just the way

she wanted it. Full of love, lots of laughing and *lots* of music. The sound of a choir brings real good memories for me. I got a little caught up."

"I don't hold it against you at all. A mass choir *and* Queen Whitney? Turn up!"

"Joy to the world, indeed."

He looked around, then grabbed the single guest chair and took a seat. He hadn't even broken a sweat. And he was close enough, when he leaned forward and rested his elbows on his knees, for me to tell.

"I hope you don't mind that I came to your office. Anthony said you like for people to call. But I also noticed you don't pick up the phone when he calls."

I pulled my desk chair back so I could sit. "Anthony and I... well, we have a unique relationship. I promise I'll be professional with you."

"I don't need any special treatment. I just don't want to bother you."

"You're not a bother, Booker. Really."

"Okay, then." He smiled, then nodded.

"Okay then. So... you came up here for something?"

He flipped the folder open. I recognized the account profile for Henderson Mechanics, an auto repair shop with locations all over Georgia, Florida and Alabama. "I was talking with Victor Henderson today and he asked me to check on a few application functions that he thinks he should have access to. Anthony dipped out a few days ago, but I saw your car in the parking lot—"

I clicked a few keys, bringing up the Henderson account in the Precision database. "What can I help you with?"

We reviewed Victor's questions and requests, and I detailed the features that would become available to his shops as he increased his subscription rate. Henderson was still small potatoes compared to Napa Auto and their counterparts, but his goal was to have black owned repair and auto parts shops nationwide. Precision Systems Software aimed to grow with him every step of the way.

"He can have these features tomorrow, if he wants them. All of them are enabled, just not at the level of service he's paying for. If he wants to upgrade, which Anthony has been trying to talk him into for years, he'll have the full software suite and it'll open up capabilities for him."

Booker relaxed in the chair as well as he could relax in an uncomfortable side chair, folding his arms across his chest. "Years, you said. Anthony is a damn good salesman. If this was a money thing, he would have wrapped this up."

"Anthony seems to think it's about money and Victor being cheap. I don't, though," I said, shaking my head. "Victor is about my dad's age. Mid sixties, doing well for himself. He could stay comfortable if he doesn't make any moves, makes it work with what he's got. Or..."

"He could stretch a little, take a risk, and see how it plays out. Then this becomes a matter of showing him how taking a leap could make his good life better. A little investment could bring him a nice payback and then some."

"Exactly. And that you picked right up on that? Tells me you're just the man for the job. Not that Anthony isn't. He's just motivated by something entirely different."

I flipped the folder closed and handed it to him. He took it, but his brown eyes bore into mine. "I guess I know how that feels to face that choice. I know how good it is on the other side of that jump."

"I guess you do. So use that, Booker."

"Excellent advice. So uh..."

He tucked the folder under his arm and gave no indication that he was planning to leave my office soon. Which was fine, because while I wasn't fond of in-person visits, I wasn't in a hurry for him to leave.

"So... uh...." I prodded, hiking my brow up a bit.

"Well, the other night, you mentioned that you knew of some spots around here where we could grab a bite. I kind of dropped you in a rude way, and I feel bad about that. I hoped that I could take you up on that raincheck."

My mouth formed a perfectly round O. I hadn't expected him to bring up the other night. I blushed internally at the way I fumed and stomped away from him, then called Faith and wrangled a dinner invite so I could bitch all night about the man that wouldn't ignore a phone call to go to dinner with me.

"I know it's last minute, but it's still early and I'm hungry. Since you're here, you must be too. Unless you had plans and you were just sticking around to meet up with someone."

I waved a hand, dismissing that. I'd normally be out of the door at four thirty and perched up at one of my favorite haunts — a hotel lobby, a dive bar for trivia night, or one of the casual eateries near my condo. More often than not, I'd be trying not to yawn in the face of someone who thought he was impressing me with his sports car or his designer suit or his Egyptian silk socks, meanwhile hoping he was packing enough to make the evening worth my time.

Since my conversation with Faith and Anthony, I hadn't been interested in hanging out at my usual places in my Hot Girl Gear, trying to make do with the same old same old. I was, honestly, going to try to be better about paying attention to men who were paying attention to me.

Like the one sitting in my office.

"I'm starving, actually. But I have quiche and a green salad waiting for me at home."

"Quiche? Salad?" His face crinkled up, and he sneered, tilting his head so he was giving me the side-eye. "When you could have ribs... or whatever?"

"Well, Faith's party is tomorrow and I have a system. I keep it light the night before, that way I can act a fool at her table. I know some people will be wearing their New Year's Eve best. I'm wearing my nicest pair of leggings, if that gives you any hint at the ridiculous amount of food I plan to eat."

"She's that good of a cook? Hmmm. I might need to follow your lead. Not tonight, though. I'm crazy hungry."

Booker pushed a soft, sexy groan through pursed lips and stood, moving toward the door. He slapped the folder against his thigh and raised a hand in a wave. "I guess I'll see you tomorrow."

Then he was gone, already headed down the hall toward the elevators. In a split second, I hopped up and hurried around my desk.

"Booker!" I called to his retreating back. He stopped and turned.

He'd only made it a few doors down the hall, so I walked toward him and he closed the space between us.

"You're welcome to join me. For quiche. I live close."

He chuckled, wrapping one large hand around the opposite wrist. "No offense, Sienna, but quiche and salad isn't going to cut it for me. Appreciate the offer, though."

"Well, wait! I know my way around a Door Dash menu. We could order some ribs... or whatever."

"Alright, okay. Twist my arm," he said, giving in entirely too easily and much to my delight. I grinned, feeling victorious. It was looking like a boring night for the girl, but things were looking up. "Whereabouts do you live?"

* * *

My condo was down the street from Booker's apartment complex. In recent years, mixed-use developments had sprung up, surrounding Precision Software and other businesses in downtown Alpharetta, Georgia, an Atlanta suburb. Acres of retail, entertainment, and housing had created the perfect live-work-play footprint, bringing more residents and employers to the area. Most of the staff at Precision lived in one of the apartments or condos just a few miles from the office.

I'd shut my system down and rushed home right after Booker agreed to have dinner with me. I'd hardly been home to do more than sleep, eat and change clothes all week, so the place was looking as clean as the Merry Maids staff had left it the week before.

I flipped the switch so that the pearl lights on the Christmas tree and around the windows glowed. I lit a few peppermint candles and positioned the plethora of red velvet bows that I'd put up in various spots throughout the place just right.

Just before three firm knocks sounded at the door, I cued up my Holiday Soul playlist. The O'Jays, White Christmas wafted from the speakers as I pulled the door open.

Booker was on the other side, wearing the same thing he'd worn to work, but he'd gone home first, too. His goatee had been cleaned up, his skin glowed, his low cut looked freshly brushed.

"You found me. Come on in."

I stepped back and let him in, sucking in a scent I recognized — Coach Platinum. It enveloped him, tingeing the air with a spicy, manly aroma. He handed me a bottle of

Veuve Clicquot while he shrugged off a worn leather jacket.

"Precision must pay nice at your level. I looked at a model of these condos, but I decided they were too pricy right now."

"So you spent the extra money on champagne?" I laughed, taking the bottle, then I took his jacket and hung it on a hook near the front door.

"I couldn't show up empty handed," he said. "Nah, I got that from my realtor, when I finally decided on an apartment. I don't really drink champagne. I figured you could probably find more reasons to drink it than I could."

"You figured right. Thanks for the hand-me-down."

I waved him down the hallway and past the kitchen to the living room. "I bought this unit ten years ago and did little updates here and there. The investors that own the property started renovating the units a few years ago. If I want mine updated, I have to move out for four months."

I set the bottle of champagne on the coffee table next to a bright red poinsettia and dropped onto the couch, exhaling a long, loud sigh. "Make yourself comfortable," I told him.

He did so, having a seat on the cushion next to me. He stretched his long legs, crossing them at the ankles under the coffee table.

"How are you liking Precision so far? I hope they're taking good care of you. Even though they make us wear ugly shit like this sweater."

He glanced at my sweater and burst into laughter like he hadn't noticed it earlier. It was an oversize blue knit with a macrame gingerbread house and two candy canes on the front of it.

"Precision is alright so far. It's... different."

He paused, an odd expression clouding his face. But then the cloud dissipated, and he smiled, pointing to my sweater. "You know, you don't have to participate in these things. Kwanzaa lunches and themed clothing days. Zo can't fire you for not wearing an ugly sweater."

"Oh, I know. It's a solidarity thing. I can't stand her chummy, *we're a team* bullshit, like she doesn't make a smooth hundred grand more a year than I do." I huffed, rolling my eyes. "But our community, the software industry especially, has so few Black woman CEO's. I want Zoraya to topple all the tech bros, so I'll throw my support behind her. To a point."

"So you're not gonna Wobble with me at the company picnic next year?"

"I didn't say that. I am the Wobble queen!"

"Aight. In the meantime, I promise not to harass you about going to potluck lunches and other corporate schmooze bullshit. And I know that's supposed to be an ugly sweater, but... it looks mighty cute on you. So you win anyway."

"Thanks. That's sweet of you to say." My heart thumped wildly under said ugly but cute sweater. I didn't know if he was flirting or just being nice, but I never turned down a compliment.

I sat up, reaching for the MacBook that had been sitting on the coffee table. "We'd better order something for you, or it'll take all night to get here. Did you really want ribs?"

"Or whatever," he answered, scooting so closely that his shoulder smashed into mine. My kryptonite was a good smelling man and his cologne danced on my nerve endings in a delicious way. "You live around here. What do you recommend?"

"Uh..." I clicked around my Door Dash account,

bringing up my recent history. "Smokestack is really good. Cue is good, too. For ribs... or whatever."

I glanced up, realizing too late that our faces were inches apart. My gaze met his and for a few seconds, we both froze, fully aware that the moment could go either way. I fancied myself a modern woman that went for what she wanted, so I was never opposed to making the first move, but this time, my gut told me to hang back. Let him decide which way he wanted to go.

Booker leaned in and my breath hitched in my throat. My eyes reflexively closed, but when his lips didn't gently press themselves against mine, they fluttered open again. He was flipping through cards in his wallet.

"Is Smokestack the best you ever had? Like... I'm in the mood for some *good* food."

I shrugged, trying to come back from embarrassment and failing miserably. He wasn't going to kiss me. He was pulling his wallet from his pocket. My face was in flames and I was hot, like someone had turned the temperature in my condo to 103 degrees.

"They're really good," I pushed out. "Cue is better, but they're slow."

"You sound like you know what you're talking about, so I'll let you pick."

He handed me an American Express black card and flipped his wallet closed. "Order something for yourself. Quiche and salad, my ass. Make sure we get some bread."

Chapter 9

Booker

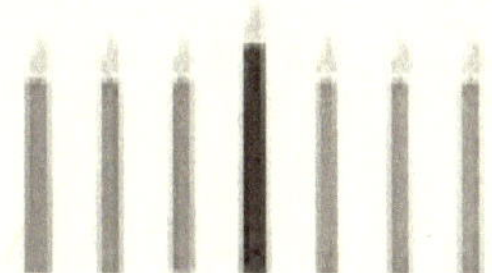

B**ooker**

Sienna went with Cue, but as promised, they were moving slowly, so she cut a few slices of that quiche I had talked shit about and warmed them up. It was savory, with spinach and onions and a flaky crust. It wouldn't do much to satisfy my hunger, but it was tasty.

We ate and chatted while we waited for *actual* dinner to arrive.

"So, you've been at Precision for a minute. A lot of people job hop these days. I have. You must really like it."

"I do," Sienna said, before a forkful of food disappeared

into her mouth. She chewed, then swallowed. "I guess I like the field. It's cutting edge, you know? The engineers work hard to not only keep up with the competition, but to best them. To offer capabilities that nobody else is doing."

"We definitely have more potential for growth than Double-X. I wish I could tag team Anthony's area with him. He's a force."

"He is. He's good at his job. He is a pain the ass, but... by now, I can't imagine not working with him."

I'd scraped the last of the egg dish from my plate but was still hungry. I glanced up at the clock to see how long I had to last before our delivery would have arrive.

"You two seem close. Is that the long friendship talking? Or the years of working together?"

"Both, I guess. We've learned how to manage our friendship and our work relationship. You'll develop a relationship with your analyst too. They're designed to be your right hand, your go-to. I know Anthony's — well, your accounts now—better than he knows them because I'm in the files every day."

"Tell you the truth..."

I regretted even starting that sentence and knew to my core that I shouldn't finish it. My attraction to Sienna was about to get me in trouble. Again. But it wasn't like I could suck the words back in.

Ah, well. I was a big boy. I could probably handle one more heartbreak.

"Tell you the truth," I started again, "I'd love it if I could keep you on my accounts. I don't want to have to invent reasons to come to your office."

"And... you'd want to come see me?"

"Yeah. Like, every day."

After a few beats, she asked, "For like... work reasons?"

"Or whatever," I answered. "Inside those doors at Precision, your demeanor says *go away*. You have this antisocial thing going, like that mean mug you had on when I met you in the elevator."

"In my defense, I was grumpy because Anthony made me come downstairs."

"And that hoodie you wear that says *fuck off*..."

She cackled. "Faith gave me that hoodie! It does not say fuck off, Booker!"

"You don't seem like you'd *want* someone to come see you." I chuckled and so did she. "You're a tough nut, Sienna. You... require work. I suppose I like a challenge. A puzzle. I don't know, maybe that's my problem."

"Your problem?" She asked. At the same time, the doorbell chimed. And, right on time, because I was a little too warm, a little too comfortable, and getting a little too close to opening up to Sienna.

I got up and followed her to the door, grabbed the bag from the delivery guy and slipped him a nice bill. He smiled in surprise. "Happy holidays to you."

I fist bumped the young man and watched him bounce down the hall with some pep in his step. When I walked back inside, Sienna closed the door, then glanced up at me.

"You know you can tip on the app, right?"

"Yeah. But my boy Ryan works weekends for a food delivery service. He doesn't always get his tips, so I like to give cash. That guy is running his own business. Down with capitalism."

Sienna laughed, following me back down the hall. "Alright, as we get ready to eat a meal made possible by a capitalist society and delivered by the employee of a wealthy corporation."

She paused in the kitchen and grabbed a couple of clean plates, silverware and napkins.

"Your life is about to change, Booker. Cue is an experience."

* * *

"When you said experience, I was expecting good. That..."

I wiped my mouth, then my brow, then tossed the napkin onto my decimated plate. I would have licked the sauce off of the porcelain, but I wanted Sienna to still be impressed with me.

"It's amazing, isn't it?"

"Otherworldly. I halfway wanna call them back, cuss 'em out for being so good and order more food, just to be greedy."

"Well, they're not going anywhere. And now you know about Cue. Next time we'll try Smokestack and you can compare and contrast."

"Next time? You're gonna let me enjoy your presence one more time?"

"Booker..." She giggled, slapping my arm. "Stop that. If I didn't want you here, you wouldn't be here."

"Is that so?" She bobbed her head in a nod. "Because I bought you dinner?"

"I don't date men for dinner. I can buy me dinner. Breakfast, lunch, brunch, linner—"

"What the fuck is *linner*? Sound like some shit college girls made up."

"Some shit Faith and I made up in college, smart ass. It's the meal between lunch and dinner. It made us feel better about having a bowl of noodles in the middle of the afternoon. Especially after that two o'clock government class freshman year."

"You know, that's one thing I missed out on?" I clicked my tongue. "College friends."

"Old friends are old friends. You mentioned Ryan... where'd you meet him?"

"Work," I answered. "All my close friends, I met through various jobs. Dishwasher, line cook, construction. It was just me and Meemaw for a long time. I didn't win any scholarships for college, and social security only goes so far. She definitely couldn't pay for it, though she wanted to. I worked to help keep the lights on. And when..."

I stopped talking. Because... why? Why was I telling my business to this woman? We worked together. I didn't know her and she didn't know me. I didn't want her interest in me to be based on a sob story.

"When..." Sienna prodded, reaching to grab her half empty glass of water and sinking back into the soft cushions on the overstuffed couch. "I'm nosy, so I'm here to listen, if you want to talk, but you don't have to."

She scooted closer, eyes wide. My mouth just... fell open.

"When she started not being able to breathe, not being able to regulate her heartbeat, things got serious. Doc diagnosed her with heart failure. I needed to be able to pay for care that Medicaid didn't cover. So I went out and hustled. I did some odd jobs, but my main job was at Double-X, working in customer care for a while."

Sienna nodded. "You showed potential, so they moved you up, huh? They make great salesmen."

"Because we know the customer and how the software works. Anyway, yeah. I moved up quick, first to tech support, and then sales. And uh... I met this woman. Boss' daughter. She... was a lot."

"Is *a lot* a code for *bitch who destroyed your life?*"

"I actively participated in destroying my life like a clown. I wanted to take care of my grandmother, make her comfortable. Tara's father owns Double-X Systems. He made her work there, I guess so he could keep an eye on her."

An eyebrow hiked up at the mention of Tara's name. I'd said it that night on the phone, when I had to beg off of dinner with Sienna. A dinner I should have taken her up on, instead of arguing with Tara.

"Yeah," I said, confirming the unasked question. "*Her*. Tara's father wouldn't support her if she didn't work for him. She could get a job or whatever, but if she needed money from Daddy, she had to work at Double-X. They had some kind of deal where if she got married, he would give her a lump sum of money. So, she floated this plan to make her dad think she had fallen in love, that we were engaged. Then she gets the lump sum, and we split it. I have money to take care of my grandma, and she has enough money to never bother her father again in life. So, I went for it. And we almost pulled it off."

"Booker..." She smacked her forehead. "No...."

"Trust me, that's what all of my friends said. Meemaw, too. She was real disappointed."

"So how did it end up? Were you foiled by some kids and a dog in a mystery van?"

"Dupree figured out the scam after we got married."

"Well, how long did you fake date her?"

I laughed. "A couple of months. And it wasn't *fake* dating, per se. We dated, we had fun, we had sex. But we weren't in love and that shit wasn't gonna last forever."

"But... he paid for a wedding and everything?"

"Hell no. We went to the courthouse and got married. Tara and her dad went back and forth about the money for almost a year. She changed her name to mine, moved me into her apartment, trying to convince him we were *actually* married.

"One day, Dupree walked into my office and shut the door. He sat in that chair and said he was going to level with me, that we both knew she scammed me. He asked me what it would take to get me to walk away. I told him about my grandmother, what I needed the money for. Meemaw was real sick by this point, and I was working like crazy to pay hospital bills. She needed an oxygen tank and regular delivery and so many medications..."

Slowly, I wagged my head. It had been a long time since I laid the whole story out. Once I started talking, no matter how fantastic and outrageous it sounded, I couldn't stop.

"He cut me a deal. He would let her think she'd get something if she annulled our marriage. We were still within an allowable time frame and considering the entire thing was a scam, we would have no problem getting a judge to sign the order. If I signed those papers, he would pay me a lump sum. And I would just... walk away."

I shrugged. "I guess if I was in love with her, I would have been offended. But it had been a long year of being married to her and not getting the benefit that I had married her for. She obviously felt the same; she had the papers drawn up. I signed. Dupree walked in with a check just as she was signing and handed it to me. When she realized I was getting paid? She blew up."

"Wow." Sienna's jaw had dropped lower and lower, the more of my story I told. I wouldn't have believed it either, if

I hadn't lived it. "How *toxic*. What a fucked up relationship with your father."

"Dupree wants her to be someone else's problem, but he also wants control of her. She wants to be independent, but she also wants Daddy's money. They play these games with each other, and I somehow got mixed up in it. The entire family is a bowl of nuts. I'm happy to not be related to those folks anymore."

"It's weird knowing inside information like that. Like... *that's* who is running that company? How are they doing so well?"

I shook my head. "How Double-X does the numbers it does is a mystery. It's good software, but they're set to topple. A feather could knock them over."

"Well, we're about to topple them, aren't we?" Sienna winked at me.

I laughed. "We?"

"Yes, we. As in Precision. Right?"

"Right. *We*."

"Lemme ask you something though, Booker..."

She paused, waiting for my eyes to flick back up to hers. "Do you think there's another kind of *we* happening here?"

My eyes locked onto hers. She was asking exactly what I wanted her to ask. I knew how she wanted me to answer. "What do you think?"

"Maybe I'm hoping so? But I'm asking, to be clear, because you might have workplace drama PTSD."

I laughed at that. "I definitely hope there's another kind of *we* happening here. Otherwise... my penis is at the wrong party."

She laughed, out loud, in my face. "Oh, God, no..." Her lips still bent into a sultry smile as she leaned into me. "He's at the right party."

"Sienna," I whispered, just before the distance between us closed. Just before I hit the point of no return — so long as I didn't get an objection from the other side. She froze. "You heard that whole story, and... you still want to make this move? You know what you're doing?"

"Yeah. I heard that whole story and I know exactly what I'm doing."

"The last thing I want is more workplace drama. I've had enough of that. I sense that you're a grown woman who can handle her business. And I don't *think* you're trying to scam me. I can't... *not* be interested in you, Sienna. But Anthony told me—"

"Anthony looks out for me, like an overbearing big brother should. I understand his concern, because we work for the same company. But yeah... I'm grown. And so are you. And it's just you and me right now. He told me that I need to pay attention to men that are paying attention to me."

She moved again, so she was even closer, tucking a hand between my thighs and gripping my length through my jeans.

"Are you paying attention to me, Booker?"

A slow smile crept across my lips. "Parts of me are paying very close attention to you, Sienna."

Chapter 10

Sienna

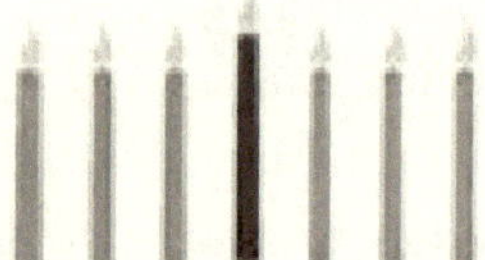

S ienna

If I'd had the time, or for that matter, any spare brain waves to think about it, I'd have found it ironic that the man that Anthony insisted wouldn't be into hanging out, hoping we'd have sex ended up hanging out my place and was currently blowing. my. back. *out.*

When I'd reached for him earlier, I found what I had hoped to find — a man who was aroused and interested. I didn't know what Booker hoped to find, but he didn't seem to have a problem with full breasts and womanly curves. He took my mouth like he had been thinking about that kiss for a long time, holding back until he couldn't resist a moment longer.

In minutes, my ugly-cute Christmas sweater was on the floor, followed by his t-shirt and, now and then, another article of clothing from one or both of us. We kissed until our lips were red, raw and chapped. He nibbled on my earlobes and dropped kisses around my neckline, making his way to the rise of my breasts before taking each nipple into his mouth and flicking the tip with his tongue.

By the time we christened the living room floor, I was white hot, slick between my thighs and writhing, begging him to fuck me. We stopped to take a water break and ended up fucking up against the kitchen counter before we made it to my bedroom.

"Is there a bed under there?" Booker had joked while standing by, sheathed erection at attention, watching me toss a hundred pillows from the king sized bed to the chair next to it.

I snickered, tossing a playful glare back at him. "I like to be comfortable. And it looks cute."

"Yeah, until you gotta put a hundred pillows back on the bed."

"Well, that can be your job."

He'd made short work of picking up where we left off in the kitchen, bringing me to near orgasm in a few strokes. I grunted, my throat raw from a long night of pleasured grunting. Booker hovered above me with my legs slung over his strong shoulders, his hips crashing against mine, sometimes grinding his pubic bone against my clit before returning to deep, plunging thrusts.

"Tell me when you're coming," Booker panted, his gaze finding mine. There was fire in his eyes. I sensed by the trembling in his limbs and the way his nose flared that he was on the edge.

I brought my legs down and reached for him, bringing his face down to mine until we were pressed together, chest to chest. I hooked my heels behind his thighs and rolled my hips up and into his while kissing him, sucking on his tongue.

He broke the kiss, moaning, "Fuck, Sienna...."

His strokes quickened to match my rhythm. I gushed at the sound of my name being moaned in the throes of passion. The first curls of orgasm wound through me, starting in the small of my back. My body began its pre-climax arch.

He dipped his head long enough to press his lips to mine in a fevered kiss before tucking a hand behind my neck and anchoring his body with a fist. His long, hard thrusts returned, pounding his body into mine.

"Booker! Yeah! Right... right there!"

I chanted his name and some other sounds that were incoherent, even to me. I felt flush, red-hot and my pussy pulsed, squeezing and contracting around him, which sent Booker over the edge immediately after.

His head cocked back, and he sucked in a long, loud breath while his body quaked. When he was spent, he collapsed on top of me, then managed to scoot over so he was only halfway lying across my body. The room was cool, but sweat beaded up on his skin like he'd run a mile in the desert.

"That... was..." Booker was still out of breath. I hadn't quite caught up on my air intake either.

"Best sex of my life," I declared.

"Something like that. Yeah."

"That's what you were going to say, right?" I rolled my

head in his direction. "Not that this was a mistake, or anything? That we shouldn't date... or even occasionally fuck, because we work together?"

"Mmmmm." He pretended to think, then shook his head. "Nah. I was going to say that tonight was the most fun I have had in a longer time than I want to admit. And that I want to do all of that, all over again. A lot. And that we should definitely, more than occasionally, fuck."

He stretched far enough to brush his lips across mine. "And that you should warm me up some more of that quiche in a minute."

"Booker.... seriously. If you need an out, you can take it."

This was where and when every instinct told me to run. To guard my heart, because I only had one. This was where I threw up the wall and dared someone to climb over it. This place, this point, these feelings that coursed through me... they weren't unfamiliar. They weren't even unwelcome. But they made me nervous.

I don't like feelings.

Booker flipped over onto his back, grabbing two of the pillows I'd left on the bed to prop behind his head. He opened his arms, and I sat up, molding myself up against his body. The muscles in his arms rippled as he closed them around me.

"I don't want an out, Sienna. I had a taste of what it was like to belong to someone. To take care of someone. To be taken care of. I want that, but for real. I said earlier that you require work. I've got my hard hat. My work boots. I've never been scared of work."

He dipped his head, bringing his lips to mine. I met him halfway, opening my mouth to deepen the kiss. When he pulled back, he grinned down at me.

"What would have happened if Anthony had let you be antisocial the other day?"

"We wouldn't have had to sit through that raggedy Kwanzaa brunch."

I felt Booker's laugh through his chest. "And that ugly ass cake."

"I'm already looking forward to the Spread the Love lunch for Valentine's Day. I hope Zo finds a new cake recipe."

Booker groaned.

I laughed. "Oh my God, this is going to be fun."

Booker

Booker

Sienna pried me from her bed about an hour before we were due to show up at Anthony's house. I had to roll home, shower and change my clothes, so she came to my place and we would leave from there.

I showed her around the sparsely decorated apartment, ignoring her mutterings of *bachelor* this and *single guy* that. Her place was decorated to the nines. I told her she could help me get my place together.

I got her settled in the living room with the TV and went to my bedroom, swinging the door closed behind me and headed to the bathroom. In the pocket of my jeans, my nearly dead phone buzzed. I pulled it out, using one hand to turn on the shower head and scrolling with the thumb of another.

Calls upon calls upon calls from Tara. "You know what?" I muttered to myself. "Let's dead this right now." I clicked my tongue, then opened her contact card. I tapped *block this caller,* then tapped save.

Then I went back to my call history and text messages and deleted every call and message from Tara. I was officially moving on.

Next up: WhatsApp.

Booker: Head.

Greg: Ayyy. You just saying hey, or you serious?

Booker: Yes. To both. *high five emoji* And that's all I have to say about that.

Jordan: What's going on in here? Booker got head?

Ryan: What up, Book?

Booker: Let's just say Tara is officially part of my past. I'm about to shower and hit this NYE party with my new girl.

Ryan: Go off, young man. We get details later though, right?

I laughed aloud.

Booker: I think Sienna would be as happy about that as Nalah and Ayanna would be. So ask yourself that question again... let me know what answer you come up with.

Jordan: Sucker. Pussy whipped ass sucker.

Booker: Happy to join the ranks of the likes of you and Ryan. I gotta bounce. I'll tell y'all more later, but she's mad cool. And guess where she works? LOL.

Ryan: BOOKER.

Greg: Fuck is wrong with you, man?

Jordan: Somebody didn't learn his lesson.

Booker: For real, though... I actually like Sienna. I'm serious, she's cool. I told her all about Tara, the whole story.

Ryan: And still... head?

Booker: I gotta go. Y'all not gonna get me in trouble

Booker: But yeah.

Jordan: *reggae horns*

Greg: I gotta get dressed. First date tonight. Hopefully I'll have Book's luck.

Booker: Ay, y'all have a good night. This is gonna be a great year.

Ryan: Back atcha, fool.

* * *

Sienna and I stood at the door of a sprawling home with perfectly cut emerald green blades of grass, stark white shutters around each window, and stately columns along the front porch. We were late, and it was my fault, and I didn't regret a second of why. I'd come out of the shower to find Sienna sprawled across my bed and I couldn't resist one more taste, so by the time we arrived, the street was lined with cars and the sounds of a party well underway filtered to my ears.

"I look okay?" I tugged at the sleeve of my button-down shirt, open at the collar. I wore a lightweight wool vest over it and a new pair of jeans with sneakers.

"Don't worry about it," said Sienna. "I'm literally wearing a sweater and leggings."

She looked cute though, in a cropped red sweater, skin tight leggings that made her curves pop and thigh high flat boots. I had enjoyed taking those off of her earlier in the day. I would enjoy taking them off again later that night.

The front door swung open, the sounds of music and laughter spilling out of the opening. Anthony wore almost exactly what I was wearing, only a different shirt and vest. I immediately felt better about my attire.

He had opened his mouth to say something, but froze as he took in the sight of Sienna and I. Together. Holding hands and probably radioactive, the afterglow was so potent.

Then his smile returned. "Figures. The minute I told him he couldn't have you, and said you couldn't have him, I knew you two would defy me and find each other. See? Matchmaking. I know what I'm doing."

"Whatever, Cupid," Sienna said, brushing past him.

I bumped fists with him, but he grabbed my arm to hold me back. "You know what I gotta say, right?" I gave him a deep nod. I'd been expecting the *if you hurt her, I'll hurt you* speech. "Alright. Have fun. Be good."

Sienna introduced me around to her friends — Faith, Will and his wife Saidah, who were the talk of the evening because not only did they meet at the Thomas house, but had recently married, and Saidah was sporting a baby bump. I shook hands with more than a few other friends from their college days and a couple of people I recognized from Precision.

The star of the show was the buffet. It was covered in food, including a little crock pot of red beans and rice. Faith took me aside to tell me she had a to-go portion already set aside for me. I fell in love with her on the spot.

Once I ventured past the buffet, I found food everywhere. The kitchen bar and every side table had samplings of a different dish, plus punch and every kind of drink imaginable. I now understood why Sienna had worn leggings and told me to pace myself. I tasted everything — and I mean *everything* that Faith set out.

I would definitely join a gym.

At a quarter to midnight, I was laid out on Anthony's patio lounger, smoking a cigar and nursing a drink, staring up at the stars that twinkled above. I always felt like the stars twinkling was Meemaw saying hello.

I raised a glass to her, saying hello back.

"Booker! I've been looking for you!" Sienna came around the lounger and bent over me, I guess checking to see if I had passed out. She seemed relieved that I was conscious and smiled down at me. "It's almost midnight! Are you coming in for the toast?"

I held a hand out to her, but instead of letting her help pull me up, I pulled her down to me. She giggled, lightly protesting, but then settled on my lap, leaning her head back against my chest.

"I'm cool with this moment being about me and you, Sienna. We both have some work ahead of us but like I said... I'm not scared of work. Are you?"

Sienna twisted around so we could see each other, then laid a long, juicy kiss on my lips. "Happy New Year, Booker. To a new start for both of us."

Have You Met Will & Saidah?

Saidah's Christmas memories have been warped by personal tragedy. A chance encounter brings her unexpected love and a new outlook on life. Here's to finding love where you least expect it!

Read on for a sneak peek of Unexpected, a holiday short.

THE GREATEST ACT OF COURAGE IS NOT FALLING IN LOVE BUT, DESPITE EVERYTHING, FALLING IN LOVE AGAIN
- ROBIN WAYNE BAILEY

Chapter 1

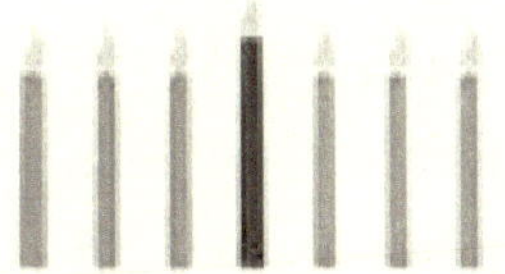

"Merry Christmas!" Faith bellowed as soon as she opened the door. She had a toddler perched on one hip and a shy four-year-old behind her legs.

I stepped into the house, my heels clicking on the marble inlay. Anthony did very well as a software consultant and Faith's catering business added to the pot. The Thomas family lived very well, in a near-palatial estate in affluent Alpharetta. You'd never know it by looking at them, though. They were the most down-to-earth people I had ever met, generous to a fault and always happy to lend a helping hand or a word of advice where needed.

"I'm not sure you need this wine. Sounds like you've already had enough to drink." I handed Faith the two bottles of wine I had picked up—I couldn't decide between a cabernet or merlot, so I brought both — and I took the baby from her arms.

"Can't I just be happy to see you? It's been years since you were here on Christmas. Come on in, make yourself at home."

"Wait!" I hissed at Faith before she veered off to the kitchen. "Is... is he here?"

She rolled her eyes. "Did you miss that Range Rover in the driveway? That's not mine, and you know Anthony is a Denali guy." I hadn't missed the ebony black SUV with the shiny alloy wheels hogging most of the driveway.

She set the bottles of wine near a small but growing collection of wines on the counter and reached for Avery, who nearly launched out of my arms into hers. Ashley followed closely behind her mother.

"Hello Miss Ashley, acting like you don't know me." She smiled and ducked out of sight. It always took her a minute to warm up to me. "I see you back there. We'll talk later, okay?"

Faith pushed me toward the living room with her fingertips. "Stop stalling. Go. Make a good impression."

I sucked in a deep breath and stepped down the hall

into the formal living room where Anthony was holding court near the stone fireplace, his glass half full of something dark. The tree was the focal point of the room, grandiose and glamorous, impressive in both height and decoration. Faith changed the theme and colors every year. This year the bulbs were deep ruby red satin and glittering gold that reflected the softly glowing pearl lights perfectly. The red velvet tree skirt, unfurled and surrounding the tree so elegantly, was the perfect touch.

"She outdid herself this year," said Anthony, from across the room. "Our biggest tree yet. Had to decorate half of it from upstairs."

"She is a big one," I agreed with a smile. "Merry Christmas, Anthony. Did you guys open the gifts from me?"

He nodded. "The girls love their Misty Copeland Barbies. We set them up right next to the Ava dolls. And I'm digging this G-Shock watch."

He flicked his wrist to show off the watch I'd gotten him. That didn't really go with the casual look he was going for with slacks, a long-sleeved shirt and vest, but I appreciated the sentiment.

"Faith loved the Tiffany pendant you got her. I was a little scared, because I had a blue box under the tree for her too. But I'm sure you ladies will chat about that."

"So... uh..." I glanced around the room to find it empty, save myself, Anthony and another gentleman that looked familiar, but I couldn't place him. "Where is Jay? I wanted to say hello."

"Jay had to step outside to take a phone call. He'll be right back. But this is his brother, Will."

Less than interested in some counterfeit version of Jay but not wanting to seem rude, I stepped forward and shook the hand offered to me. "Nice to meet you," I mumbled with a smile. He replied with something similar. He was handsome and looked just like his brother. He just... wasn't Jay.

The door to the patio swung open and in walked Jay, tucking a mobile phone into the pocket of a pair of dark jeans. He was a taller, broader, even more handsome version of the Jay I used to know. He wore black loafers and a grey cashmere V-neck sweater with a shirt under it, the collar unbuttoned enough to reveal the neck I used to love to plant kisses around.

"Jay. Hello. It's been a long time."

The words tumbled out of my mouth as I walked—no, *glided* across the room toward him. I extended a hand and gave him my warmest smile, which I hoped would let him know that I harbored no hard feelings toward him. I was older, wiser, more mature, a better woman than I had been so many years ago.

"Hey, what's up," he said, brushing past me. I stood there, looking like a fool, my hand still extended for more than a few seconds before spinning on my heels and turning around. I watched Jay pick up a glass and shoot back a mouthful of liquor.

"Was that who I think it was?" Will asked him.

Jay nodded. "Yeah. Yeah, it's all good. We can sign paperwork on Monday."

"Yeah? Congrats on that, bro!" Will's face lit up as he stretched an arm out to his brother. They bumped fists and made irritating grunting sounds at each other. To Anthony, Will said, "Jay here just closed the deal for us to remodel that old beat up strip mall off of Panola Road. The plan is to tear most of it down, reconfigure the interior, redo the facades. It'll be a multi-million dollar deal. Not our biggest project but our most public facing for sure."

"So..." I stepped into the room and tried to wiggle my

way into the conversation. "You two run a renovation business? Or something?"

"Yes, that's exactly what we do," answered Will. "Hunter Construction does commercial structure renovation. Like when a company buys an old, previously existing building and wants to retrofit it to a vision for the new place? They call us."

"Sounds interesting. And profitable. You must be the muscle," I purred, sidling up next to Jay, gripping his arm. It was deliciously meaty inside the soft fabric of the sweater. Jay stared at me, those dark eyes locked on mine. Then his gaze slid down until they reached my hand on his arm. He looked up at me again and stepped away, conveniently removing my touch.

"Okay if I refill?" He didn't wait for an answer; instead heading toward the expansive bar on the other side of the tree.

Confused, I shot a glance at Anthony. He shrugged and took a sip of his drink. In the corner, Jay was loudly tossing ice cubes into a glass. Will watched him for a moment, his brows furrowed deeply, before glancing at me with an apologetic smile.

I didn't bother to smile back. I turned around and stomped into the spacious kitchen where I found Faith spooning aujus over the prime rib on a festive red serving platter. In multicolored dishes around the kitchen, attractively prepared sides waited to be whisked to the buffet in the dining room. The entire room smelled delicious.

"How'd it go?" she asked, her brows high upon her forehead. I shook my head and headed toward the wine, snatching a glass from its fancy storage system.

I plucked the bottle of merlot from the collection of wines, pulled a drawer handle, retrieved the opener and went at the bottle, aggressively wrenching and twisting until the cork popped. I wasted no time in filling a bulbous glass.

"Pour me one," she ordered, carting the aromatic roast past me and depositing it on the center of the buffet. When she came back, I had a glass waiting for her, but I was working on gulping mine down.

I was fuming. Absolutely fuming.

Faith angled her head to peek around the corner as she took a sip of wine. "Did you talk to him?

"Mmmhmm!" I gulped down more wine while I cut my eyes at her, and then toward the living room.

"What's that look for? What happened?"

"I *tried* to speak to that fool. He didn't even say hello. Said, *hey what's up* and walked right past me. Then I tried again; I put my hand on his arm, paid him a nice little compliment. He looked at me like my hands were dripping with acid and moved away from me."

"He did what? Like how?"

I eyed her like Jay had eyed me, then mimicked him stepping away. She mused, sipping her wine.

"Maybe he needs to warm back up to you. Give him a little time. You're sitting next to him at dinner — plenty of time to get reacquainted."

She set down her wineglass and grabbed mine. "Help me carry this stuff to the buffet so we can sit down to eat."

Chapter 2

"So... Jay. What keeps you busy these days?"

Faith refused to move me to a different seat, despite my begging. She was convinced he just needed a hot meal and some time to warm up to me and he would be fine. I wasn't so sure about that.

"Work," he bit out. "I've been building my business for the last ten years." Then he dipped his head and stabbed at a mound of green beans, stuffing them into his mouth.

"Oh. Well, that's good. You're winning contracts, so it looks like all that work has paid off. What about in your off time? Are you still playing—"

"Nah," he said, grumbling, shaking his head. "I don't get into too much outside of gym time."

Surprised, an eyebrow shot up. I always knew him as an outgoing young man, involved in sports and myriad campus clubs. "Really? You used to play on the intramural football league. And you guys always sponsored Game Night. Remember when we'd get a bunch of board games and card games together, some drinks–"

"Ooh, those were fun," Faith said, jumping in. "I was the Scattergories Queen!"

"Yeah, well, some people grow up past their college days," said Jay, swiping the corner of his mouth with a napkin. "Some people have business to take care of and can't be running the streets like they don't have any responsibilities."

"Who's running the streets like they don't have responsibility?" I asked. "Everyone needs an outlet for relaxation and stress release. Maybe you need to pick up a hobby."

Jay paused, then slowly rolled his eyes over to me. I stared him down, daring him to step over the imaginary line in the sand I'd just drawn. "Are you trying to say something to me?"

"You seem uptight, is all I'm saying."

"I don't give a shit what you think—"

"Obviously."

"... so you can keep your opinions–"

"Jay. Saidah." Faith's voice was low but stern, and even though I was a grown woman, I knew she meant business. Then she smiled. But I saw right through that fakery. "It's Christmas. Let's not."

"Tell *her* to let's not. She's the one over here deciding what folks need." His chair scraped roughly against the hardwood floor as he pushed back. "I *need* to refill my drink."

I watched a beet-red pallor cross Anthony's complexion. "Hey, man. Take it easy on my floors. We just got them re-done last spring."

"Nobody cares about your damn floors," he mumbled, shuffling away from the table, headed toward the bar.

I eyed Faith, but she was glaring at her husband, who gave her a helpless shrug of his shoulder and wide-eyed stare.

"Uhm..." Will cleared his throat, eyeing his brother out of the corner of his eye. "The... the prime rib — it's delicious. Everything is just great. I like the macaroni and cheese. I dabble a bit in the kitchen, but this is on another level. Do you use gruyere in your bechamel sauce?"

"Yes," she said, brightening. "I do. You have quite the cultured palate. Thank you, Will." Faith graciously accepted the compliment, a smile on her lips but worry in her eyes as Jay approached the table, his glass brimming with dark liquid. He dropped into his chair and dug into his meal again.

"Yeah. It's all great." He picked up a knife and began sawing at a slice of fork tender beef, scraping against Faith's fine china. "I sure appreciate this pity meal y'all invited me to since my wife left me and moved in with some broke ass–"

"Jay," said Will, his voice at the bottom of his throat, practically growling through clenched teeth. "Take it *easy*, man."

"And the bitch is asking for fucking alimony, like I wanna pay her to *not* be married to me. Fuck her, man. She can marry that broke nigga she left me for. Let him buy her Gucci and Prada, let him pay her credit card bills."

He dropped his knife, sending a spray of Au jus across his chest. "Shit. This is fuckin' cashmere, goddammit. Why y'all got these weak ass knives for cutting meat?"

Faith hopped up from the table and sprang into action. "Take it off. I have some club soda I can treat it with and I'll put it in the steamer. Won't hurt it at all."

Jay's limbs were loose; his words slurred as he pulled the sweater over his head and tossed it at her. She took it and escaped to the laundry room. He resumed his seat in his undershirt and jeans.

I reached for my glass of wine and sipped. I sure was glad I left my calm and peaceful condo to share dinner with a drunken boor. He had the demeanor—and the capacity—of a man that had been drinking for a long time. No wonder his wife had left him. I felt like I'd dodged a bullet, myself.

"Don't care about her anyway," Jay quietly raged, before inserting a forkful of food into his mouth. "Got bitches everywhere that want to be with me. One right next to me that won't leave me alone. Hey Will," he said, his head lobbing toward his brother, across the table. "Why don't you tell her I don't date fat bitches?"

"That's just fine, Will," I responded, giving him a bright

smile. "Because I don't date sloppy drunk assholes. Excuse me."

I pushed my chair back from the table, picked up my plate and marched into the kitchen. I ran into Faith on her way from the laundry room.

"Thanks for dinner, honey. I'm out of here."

"Nooo..." Faith's eyes bugged out and reached for me, wrapping her thin fingers around my arms. "Do not leave me alone with these men! Anthony won't say anything and Jay is so damn drunk–"

"That drunk just called me a fat bitch." I grabbed my purse from the alcove next to the refrigerator where I'd left it when I came in. "I don't care how handsome he used to be or how much I thought I loved him. I'm not sitting through one more second of *that*." I jabbed my finger toward the dining room where it sounded like Jay was getting started again.

I leaned toward Faith and dropped a kiss on her cheek. "Merry Christmas. Thanks for the Gucci clutch. Can't wait to break it in. Ya'll try to have a good day."

The sound of my heels echoed up into the high ceiling as I headed toward the front door, pulled it open and started down the sidewalk toward my car. I stopped long enough to gawk at the Range Rover rudely parked diagonally across the driveway. It looked as if Jay had arrived drunk and got worse.

The front door opened, and Will stepped out, rushing down the steps. He and Jay had similar features, but obviously Will was younger. He stopped when he was a few steps from me and shoved his hands into grey-black distressed jeans. His sweater, a rich cranberry, looked nice against his lighter skin tone.

"Uh... I didn't... I'm sorry; I never caught your name."

I glared at him for a moment or two before I answered. "Saidah. Saidah Harland." As if on automatic, I offered him a hand. He took it like he was going to shake it, but he held it in his hands, stroking it between his palms. "Your brother is an asshole and a drunkard. I'm sure you know this, so why you let him jump all over me and didn't say a thing—"

"Ms. Harland... Saidah. Jay's actually my half brother, but they raised together us, so..." He lifted and lowered his shoulders in a shrug. "Anyway. That's why I came out. To apologize for him, for the way he treated you and the things he said. It was uncalled for and I should have stepped in earlier."

"Well..." My hand felt warm, enclosed in his. My body felt warm under the gaze of his espresso brown eyes. "I... thank you. For the apology. I appreciate it."

"You're not taking off, are you? Because of him?"

"I didn't want to come over here anyway, but Faith said he was coming to dinner and I thought maybe..." I shook my head, then looked down at our hands, mine still intertwined in his. "I guess you really can't go home again."

"He..." Will turned to look back at the house, like he could see through the brick exterior to the scene in the dining room. "Jay's had a rough time of it, the last few years. The business hit a rough patch and his wife got impatient with the restructure. She left last year, but as you heard, she's holding out for a ridiculous amount of alimony now that the business is doing well again."

I nodded, understanding. Not forgiving, but it helped to know where the vitriol was coming from. "I appreciate the explanation. He's still pretty loose with his mouth and I *don't* appreciate that."

"I completely understand and I'm sure when he gets

right, he'll be embarrassed at himself. But I was hoping I could make up for my brother's behavior."

I pulled my hand from his, warm as it was, and started inching toward my car. "I don't need you to make up for him. I need him to do better."

"Please. Don't... don't go. You haven't even had dessert yet and–"

"Is that another crack about my weight? What is it with you two? A woman is bigger than a toothpick and she's suddenly too fat for you?" I propped my hands on my hips and lifted my chin in defiance.

"No!" He said, almost shouted. "Saidah... no. That wasn't a crack about your weight. And not that you need me to tell you you look amazing, but... you look amazing."

His eyes skipped down my figure and back up, lingering at my chest. I lifted my hands to block his vision and glared. "I'm sorry. My brother may not be interested—actually, I think he's too drunk to be interested in anything, but I really appreciate what you've got goin' on here."

"Hunh," I grunted, eyeing him. "You're not... weird or anything, are you?"

He laughed, showing off a wide smile of straight white teeth. He had a small dimple high on his left cheek. "Uh, no. I'm not weird. I don't think I am, anyway. Faith was telling me about you before you got here. How you work with at-risk kids and volunteer at the nursery at Children's Healthcare. How you two have been friends since your first day at Albany. And how you and Jay were together for a while. He must have lost his damn mind or something, because if he let a woman like you get away he had to have been crazy."

"My sentiments exactly. All this flattery aside, I need to get going. I appreciate the apology for your brother, but there's nothing you need to do to make up for him. Have a good day, and I hope you're driving home."

I stepped back, then turned around and walked to my car. I heard sneakers on the pavement, keeping a respectful distance but still following me. I reached the driver's side door and turned to find him standing on the other side of the car.

"Take me with you."

My eyebrows shot up in complete surprise. "I'm sorry, do what?"

"Jay's miserable and I'm uncomfortable and they're his friends, not mine. And I'd like to talk to you some more."

"It's Christmas Day. Where am I supposed to be taking you?"

"Anywhere. Waffle House. The parking lot at the mall. Let's just..." He turned, glanced at the house, then turned back and winked at me. That pretty brown eye *winked at me*. "Jay will probably pass out soon, and then I'll come back and take him home. Let's escape for a while."

* * *

This is such a sweet, feel good romance. Read the rest of this love story in Unexpected, a holiday short at booksbydlwhite.com/unex pected

About the Author

Atlanta based Women's Fiction and Romance author DL White began seriously pursuing a writing career in 2011. She harbors a love for coffee and brunch, especially on a patio, but her true obsession is water-- lakes, rivers, oceans, waterfalls! On the weekend, you'll probably find her near water and if she's lucky, on an ocean beach.

When not writing books, she devours them. She blogs reviews and thoughts on writing and books at BooksbyDL-White.com. Grab a book by DL White and *#Putitinyourface.*

Also by DL White

Pick up my titles in eBook, print or audio at Booksbydlwhite.com/books.

Brunch at Ruby's, a Ruby's novel

Dinner at Sam's, a Ruby's novel

Unexpected, a holiday short

Beach Thing, a Black Diamond Romance

Elysium, a Black Diamond Vacation Romance

The Pearl, A Black Diamond Romance

Leslie's Curl & Dye, a Potter Lake Small Town Romance

Second Time Around, a Potter Lake holiday short

The Guy Next Door, a Potter Lake Small Town Romance

The Kwanzaa Brunch, a holiday short

A Thin Line

The Never List

Hey, Lover, a Second Chance Romance